Fairyland

PICTURES & POEMS

Illustrations by
Arthur Rackham • Ida Rentoul Outhwaite
Warwick Goble • Margaret W. Tarrant
Florence Anderson

Poems by
Annie Rentoul • John Milton • Alfred Tennyson

Edited by Alexandra Day

LAUGHING ELEPHANT   MMXIX

By the moon we sport and play,
With the night begins our day.
As we frisk the dew does fall,
Frolic little fairies all!
Lightly as the little bee,
Two by two and three by three;
About we go, and about go we!

A little straying Sunbeam comes to the Fairy Wood.
All the bunnies know her, dressed in dusky rose;
Golden is the water, golden is the West,
The little baby brown birds snuggle in the nest,
The bunnies cuddle closer, the trees sigh, "Hush!"

What have you found within the pool of dreams,
　　Where roses of a thousand summers blow?
What strange and lovely thing of opal gleams,
　　Secrets and tears and hopes of long ago?

O rapt and beautiful, muse for a space
　　On rainbow sphere where olden memories glow;
Then gently lay your treasure in its place
　　Back in the quiet pool of long ago.

Little fairies, dainty, sweet,
With rosy frocks and dancing feet,
Flying here and flying there,
Amongst the flowers and everywhere;
Little elves in clothes of green,
In the moonlight may be seen.

The bunnies soft and shy,
The flittermouse on wings,
The little sweet wren and I
With fairy music sing.

Three spirits made with joy
Came dashing down on a tall wayside flower
That shook beneath them, as the thistle shakes
When three gray linnets search for the seed.

Dusk of the day, and the hour to ride
Atop my broom o'er the world so wide;
Meggin, the witch, am I, am I!
Free of the earth and sky.

I rock on the rim of a sailing cloud,
The lightning laughs, and the wind sings loud;
With my scarlet mantle I wave good night –
My peaky hat puts out the light.

By a silver fountain
  In a magic hour,
Once I saw a fairy,
  Lovely as a flower;
Rainbow morning-glories
  Watched her from above,
Waterlilies peeped beneath,
  Just to show their love.

Fast as almond petals
  On a windy day,
Little white feet twinkled
  In her fairy play;
Little starry white hands,
  Frail as snowdrops small,
Tossed a colored bubble up
  For a fairy ball.

On cobwebs fine and dewy grass
So nimbly do we pass,
The young and tender stalk
Ne'er bend when we do walk;
Yet in the morning may be seen
Where we the night before have been.
.

Sweet our song, and sweet are we,
When we sing so merrily;
Listen how our music floats
To the sky in liquid notes.
Tra-la-la! O, hear them swell;
Higher, higher, up they well,
Like the bubbles from a stream,
Dancing in the sun's bright gleam.

Flower fairies, have you found them,
   When the summer's dusk is falling,
With the glow worms watching round them;
   Have you heard them softly calling?
Hundreds of them, all together,
   Flashing flocks of flying fairies,
Crowding through the summer weather,
   Seeking where the coolest air is.

So blue the night,
   The moon so silver-pale,
The pool so bright,
   So still the few great stars.
On such a night,
   So full of wonderland,

Had I no sight,
   Yet should my spirit guess,
Drinking for hours
   That music's loveliness,
By the hushed flowers
   A Fairy is at hand.

Round about a fairy ring, tra la,
Thus we dance and thus we sing, tra la
Trip and go, to and fro,
Over this flowered field, tra la.
All about, in and out,
Over this field, tra la, tra la.

Good luck befriend thee, child, for at thy birth
The fairy ladies danced upon the hearth.
And, sweetly singing round about thy bed,
Spread all their blessings on thy sleeping head.